MYSTERY of the LUNCHBOX CRIMINAL

Alison Lohans

Illustrations by Janet Wilson

Scholastic-TAB Publications Ltd.
123 Newkirk Road, Richmond Hill, Ontario, Canada

Canadian Cataloguing in Publication Data

Lohans, Alison, 1949-
  Mystery of the Lunchbox Criminal

Issued also in French under title: Y a-t-il un
voleur dans l'école?
ISBN 0-590-73367-2

I. Wilson, Janet, 1952-. II. Title.

III. Series

PS8573.053M9 1990   jC813'.54   C90-093074-8
PZ7.L64My 1990

654321   Printed in Canada   01234/9
              Manufactured by Webcom Limited

To John, with love from Mom.

**Other Shooting Star books
you may enjoy:**

Speedy Sam
 by Dorothy Joan Harris

Going Bananas
 by Budge Wilson

Contents

Chapter 1

Surprise!

"I'm HUNGRY!" said J.J. "I'm so hungry I could eat a house."

"Huh," said Derek. "What about the windows, huh? You'd chew up the glass, right, and then you'd bleed and you'd —"

"Oh, shut up," J.J. said impatiently. His stomach was growling, and it was only recess. "You'd be hungry too if all you had for breakfast was five cornflakes." It was a long story, and far too complicated to explain to Derek. But he knew there were three pieces of pineapple and ham pizza waiting in his lunchbox. That made the long wait through math and spelling worth it — sort of. "Just wait till you see my lunch," he said. "It's *deadly*."

"Huh," said Derek. "All you can think about is food, and the bell's going to ring. We never raced our cars yet."

"There's still time." J.J. fingered his remote control Z-28. He wasn't so sure about racing — not in the schoolyard. Besides, Derek liked to crash cars. J.J.'s mom had said if anything happened to the Z-28, it was J.J.'s own fault. She didn't know he'd brought it to school today. Anyway, that bully Shaun Higgins might see them and take the Z-28 away. Or do something *really* awful, like step on it.

"Hurry up!" said Derek. "You're wasting our whole recess. I won't wait for you next time. I'll race Kyle instead."

"All right, all right!" cried J.J. "I'm *ready*." He

squatted down and traced a line in the dirt. "We'll go from here to the monkey bars, OK?"

He didn't like the idea of Derek racing Kyle King. Sometimes Kyle was friends with Shaun, and when he was, he acted just as mean as the bully.

"GO!" Derek yelled, getting a head start.

But J.J. didn't say anything. Intent on his car, he pressed the button. Careful of the rock. Oops! He hadn't noticed that twig. Yikes! He'd run right over it, and that sent him off course. Derek was winning!

Out of the corner of his eye he could see Kyle watching. Uh oh! Shaun too! But he couldn't quit now. He was so hungry it was hard to concentrate — especially with Shaun watching.

The bell rang.

Relieved, J.J. scooped up his car. "Race you to the door," he said.

"Huh. Who wants to race *you*?" Derek muttered. "All you do is waste time talking about food."

J.J. ran anyway. Shaun was watching with a mean look on his face.

J.J.'s stomach growled all the rest of that morning. Once it growled so loudly that the whole class laughed.

Miss Davis just smiled at him. "Ready for lunch already, J.J.?" she asked.

J.J. felt his face getting hot. "I guess so," he said.

He was *so* hungry. If only breakfast hadn't been so late, and Dad weren't out of town at that long conference in Winnipeg. If only his baby sister Jessica hadn't knocked his bowl of cornflakes onto the floor — and there hadn't been a single speck of cereal left in the box. And then Mom got that important long-distance phone call and nobody noticed the toast was stuck in the toaster until the kitchen was filled with smoke, and then it was time to leave for school anyway.

Dreamily, J.J. thought of the pizza in his lunchbox. Mom had ordered a super-extra-large yesterday at the Italian Galleon so they'd have several meals all set to go in a hurry.

"J.J." Was that the second time Miss Davis had said his name?

"Sorry," he said. "I didn't hear you."

Miss Davis had that patient waiting look on her face. "For the third time, J.J., how do you spell *piano*?"

"*P-I-Z-Z-A*," he spelled loudly, his mouth watering at the thought. And then, when the class laughed again, he realized his mistake.

Tanya Webster was waving her hand in the air. "Miss Davis? I know it, Miss Davis. *P-I-A-N-O*."

"Showoff," J.J. muttered to himself. He checked his watch. 11:30. Then he looked at the clock on the wall. It only said 11:28. How could he possibly wait a whole 17 minutes until lunch? Didn't being hungry count as an emergency? He was so hungry he felt like he might even die! If he starved to death, would his body stay sitting in his desk, or would it fall down in the aisle? Maybe they'd have a fire drill, instead, and get to go to lunch earlier than usual.

But there was no such luck. The class had to copy each spelling word one more time in their notebooks. And then J.J. had to stay after because instead of writing *piano*, he'd written *pizza* again.

The lunchroom was noisy when J.J. walked in. He had to look hard to find Derek. And then he had to walk past Shaun and Kyle to get there. Shaun stuck his foot out in the aisle.

J.J. saw it too late. He tripped. His lunchbox went flying with a clatter. The latches opened. His Thermos rolled off in one direction. The rest of his lunch . . .

But where *was* the rest of his lunch? Where was his pizza?

There was no pineapple and ham pizza on the floor. Instead, there was an ugly, smelly pile of cigarette butts!

"*What?*" cried J.J. "Where's my lunch? Where's my pizza?"

Shaun started laughing loudly. So did Kyle.

J.J. turned to the bully. "Where's my pizza?" he demanded. "I bet you took it."

"Did not." Shaun opened his mouth wide. It smelled like peanut butter. There was even peanut butter stuck on his teeth.

"He never touched your lunch," Kyle agreed. "I was with him all morning."

J.J. blinked fast and took a deep breath. Had *Kyle* taken his pizza? He didn't dare blame these two if he didn't have proof. "It's not *fair*," he said under his breath. "I was so hungry! It's not *fair*." Quickly he turned away and wiped his eyes with his arm.

"Here, J.J." Tanya Webster was standing there, holding out half a sandwich. "You can have this."

"But I want my pizza!" J.J. said.

"What's happened here?" Finally Mr. Schmidt had noticed. "Shaun Higgins, are you responsible for this mess?"

"No, I never —"

J.J. interrupted. "Somebody stole my pizza and gave me *these*." He waved his hand at the cigarette butts. "What am I going to eat? I'm starving!"

Derek crawled under a table and came back with J.J.'s Thermos. "Think there's cigarette butts in here too?" he asked.

J.J. grabbed the Thermos. "Leave my stuff alone!" he said. He opened it and looked inside. It was full of milk, just like always. But he didn't trust it. He sniffed. It smelled like milk. But what if the person who'd substituted the cigarette butts for his pizza had put something in his milk? Like poison? He went to the sink and dumped the milk.

By the time he got back to the table, the lunch room was very quiet.

"We're going to get to the bottom of this," Mr. Schmidt was saying. "Whoever played this cruel prank on J.J. should be ashamed. How would each of you feel if *you* had found this — this disgusting mess — in *your* lunchbox? Somebody owes J.J. an apology and a lunch."

J.J.'s face got hot again. Mr. Schmidt was only trying to help, but now it was even more likely that Shaun and Kyle would be waiting for him after school — because probably they'd be blamed. Meanwhile, Ginny Chen had given him some chips, Lisa Perreault had shared her celery sticks, Michael Strongchild had offered him some milk, and somebody had put three chocolate chip-oatmeal cookies at J.J.'s place. It looked like he wouldn't go hungry after all — today. But what if the same thing happened again tomorrow? And the next day?

"I'm going to get to the bottom of this," J.J. vowed to himself.

Chapter 2

More Problems

By the end of the day J.J. was feeling better. In gym he'd been the last one to be caught in the cross-fire dodgeball game. And he'd gotten 97% on his social studies test, the best mark in class. But Derek was beginning to get on his nerves. Derek kept saying that maybe J.J.'s mom was to blame for the cigarette butts.

"I bet your mom did it," Derek said again as they were walking home. He even laughed.

Derek was taking his time about getting home, kicking a rock as he walked. Sometimes it went into lawns or people's flowerbeds.

J.J. was beginning to wish Derek would get lost — but then he'd be all alone if he met Shaun and Kyle. "I told you a million zillion times!" he burst out. "Mom put *pizza* in my lunch."

"Did you see her?" asked Derek. "Huh?"

"No," J.J. admitted. "But she'd never do a thing like that. Anyway, how could she? Nobody smokes in our house."

"*Nobody's* mom would do that," said Tanya Webster. She and her little sister Amy had been tagging along all the way. "It's too mean."

"You never know," said Derek.

"What kind of friend are you?" said J.J. "Get lost!"

Derek gave his rock a big kick and followed it across the street. Then it went down an alley. So did Derek.

At first J.J. was relieved. Leaving Amy and Tanya behind, he dodged his way down the sidewalk, pretending he was evading laser bolts that would zap his feet. It was fun. That was how he'd won the dodgeball game.

But then he started thinking about Shaun and Kyle. Without Derek around, it would be two against one, and he might end up with a bloody nose. Then Mom would get all upset because he'd been fighting.

J.J. hadn't seen Shaun or Kyle since the bell rang. Maybe they had to stay late to do some corrections. Or maybe Mr. Schmidt had figured out that they were to blame for the cigarette butts, and sent them to see Mrs. Markoski, the principal.

How could he keep the same thing from happening tomorrow? Could he convince Mom to pick him up at lunch time, and they'd go have hamburgers or something? She probably wouldn't be able to do it, though. Baby Jessica seemed to take up all the time that was left over from Mom's studying.

J.J. was almost home when, without warning, something hard cracked against his skull.

"Ow!" J.J. screamed. For a minute he closed his eyes in pain and touched the spot on his head. A lump was beginning to grow.

Not too far away, he heard laughing. Out of the corner of his eye he saw Shaun lurking behind a parked car. Was Kyle there too? He couldn't tell. J.J. took a deep breath and started to run. He could hear footsteps pounding behind him. Then there was a yell. It almost sounded like a karate yell.

J.J. turned to look. Tanya Webster was facing Shaun. She moved quickly — so quickly J.J. couldn't really tell what she did. But Shaun went flying through the air and landed hard.

"I saw what you did, Shaun Higgins," she shouted. "You're always so mean it makes me sick. So you'd better think twice next time."

"Huh?" Derek had appeared from somewhere. He stood there staring.

"Look out!" J.J. yelled as Shaun picked up another rock.

"Don't try it," Tanya said in a menacing voice. "I'm almost up to black belt, you know."

"You couldn't be," Shaun scoffed. "You're a girl."

"Want to find out?" Tanya invited.

Shaun made an ugly face at her. But as Tanya began advancing toward him, he dropped the rock.

"Hey! You kids!" somebody yelled. "Quit that fighting!"

J.J. looked down the street. Mrs. Peterson was coming. She was big and had a voice that carried like the city's tornado warning siren. She looked like she could pick Shaun up by the scruff of his neck and toss him into a garbage can. When Mrs. Peterson said something, everybody listened.

"We were just having a little fun," said Shaun in a whiny voice.

"Some fun," muttered J.J.

"Shoo!" said Mrs. Peterson. "We don't need any rocks thrown here, thank you. I'll be very happy to let your parents know about this escapade."

"I was just leaving anyway," Shaun said.

J.J. looked at Tanya, still startled by what he'd seen.

"See you later, J.J.," Tanya said with a wave.

Derek was still standing there staring.

When J.J. got home the car wasn't in the driveway, and the door was locked. "Figures," J.J. said as he dropped down on the front steps to wait. He couldn't help feeling mad at his mom. He touched the painful lump and winced. Ow! Sometimes it seemed as if Mom didn't care much about him any more. All she ever did was study and look after Jessica.

Finally, the familiar yellow car rolled into the driveway. "You're late," J.J. said as his mother was getting the baby out of her car seat. "It's after 4:30."

"I'm sorry, J.J.," his mom said with a tired smile. "I had to take Jessica to the doctor and we had a long wait." She gave him a quick hug. "You had to wait outside all this time. I'm sorry." Then she noticed the bump on his head. "J.J., what happened? Have you been fighting?"

"Shaun hit me with a rock," he said.

His mom's mouth went into an angry straight line. As she lifted Jessica out of the car, J.J. noticed a red smear around his baby sister's mouth. Had Jessica had a treat, too? While Shaun was bullying him?

"Aren't you going to say anything?" J.J. demanded. "I got hit in the head with a rock. Don't you even care? I bet you don't care about my lunch either." He stomped up the front steps.

"J.J.!" Mom said sharply. "Just give me a minute to get Jessica inside. She has a fever and I need to put her to bed. Then we'll talk about it, all right?"

Jessica started crying.

"Oh boy," said J.J., and covered his ears. He felt like kicking the door, but decided he'd better not. Instead, he looked at his watch. One minute passed. "OK," he said. "A minute's up."

"J.J.!" Mom yelled. "I won't have you behaving like this. Go to your room until I call you."

J.J. pounded up the stairs. He made sure it was good and loud so Mom would hear. What was he supposed to do? Practically the whole day had been a disaster, and all she had time for was the baby. And her books. Well, maybe *one* thing hadn't been a disaster. It had been pretty awesome when Tanya sent Shaun flying. He wished he could see her do it again. Maybe he could talk Mom into letting him learn karate too.

At last his mom knocked on his door. "J.J.?" she said softly.

"What?" J.J. was lying on his stomach on his bed.

Mom came in and sat beside him on the bed. "I'm sorry about all the trouble you had after school," she said. "We'd better figure out a safe place to keep a key so you can let yourself in."

"Did Jessica get a treat?" J.J. asked. "Her mouth had red around it."

Mom sighed. "It was medicine, J.J. For her fever. She spat some up."

"Probably you don't want to hear about my

lunch," J.J. muttered.

"What about your lunch?" asked Mom. "How was the pizza?"

"There wasn't any pizza in my lunch!" J.J. yelled. "It was just full of cigarette butts, and you don't even care!"

"*What?*" cried Mom. "I gave you three pieces of pizza and your milk and an apple, and two carrot sticks. What happened to your lunch?"

"How am I supposed to know?" he yelled. "I went into the lunch room. Shaun tripped me. My lunchbox fell and spilled. All that was there was cigarette butts and my Thermos."

Mom rubbed her forehead. "This is all very confusing. You tell me your lunchbox was full of cigarette butts? How could that be? What did you have to eat?"

J.J. told her. He knew she wasn't the guilty person.

Man, that was a rotten thing to do — stealing a guy's lunch! He'd have to catch the criminal. No way was he getting a lunchbox full of cigarette butts again.

Chapter 3

The Criminal at Work

At morning recess the next day, instead of racing cars, J.J. and Derek ran to the far corner of the playground, behind the concrete tunnels.

"Wasn't that awesome?" J.J. gasped. "Tanya Webster throwing Shaun down like a piece of cardboard!"

"Yeah!" Derek's eyes sparkled. "Man, I wish

I could do that!"

"Me too!" J.J. checked over his shoulder to make sure nobody else was listening. "I've got pizza for lunch again," he said. "And a foolproof plan."

"Huh," said Derek. "How can you be sure?"

"Easy," said J.J., although suddenly he wasn't so sure any more. "I taped my lunchbox shut. If anybody gets into it, I'll be able to tell."

"Huh," said Derek. "They could still take your pizza."

A cold feeling twisted around in J.J.'s stomach. Derek was right. "Well," he said, "it would be simpler to take a lunchbox that *wasn't* all taped shut. And I thought about it all night. Whoever took my pizza probably did it at recess. Miss Davis is always in the room before school, but at recess she goes to the staff room."

"Maybe Miss Davis did it," Derek pointed out.

"That's dumb," said J.J. "Besides, she doesn't smoke. Anyway, nobody's allowed to smoke at school, not even the teachers."

"Who cares?" said Derek. "Look, are you going to waste our whole recess talking about your lunch?"

J.J. was getting impatient. "But it could happen again!" he said. "It could happen to *your* lunch, don't you see? We've got to catch the criminal!"

"What criminal?" asked Derek.

J.J. started fidgeting with an elastic that he had in his pocket. He wished Derek were more interested. "The Lunchbox Criminal!" he burst out. "We've got to catch him."

"Catch *Shaun* is more like it," said Derek. "What makes you think I'd want to catch *him*?"

Derek had a point. "Well . . . " J.J. thought fast. "Maybe Tanya could help." And then he remembered. "Shaun was outside all recess yesterday."

Derek wrinkled his forehead. "Huh. You're right. Yeah, you're right."

"I know! We should spy on the classroom," J.J. said, and took off running. He ran past Tanya, who was jumping rope on the pave-

ment. "Hey!" he cried as he peered through the classroom window. "Somebody's *in* there!"

"Where?" Derek pressed his nose against the glass. "Oh! *Wait!* Is that *my* lunchbox he's messing with?" He raced for the door.

J.J. stayed a moment longer to watch. But the person inside had obviously heard their voices. Quickly he put the lunchbox back on the shelf and slipped out of the room.

His heart pounding, J.J. sank down to a crouching position. *Think!* he told himself. Who was it?

It certainly hadn't been Shaun Higgins. In fact, he couldn't be sure if it was anybody he knew — and he knew the names of most of the kids in school. All he'd seen was the criminal's back, with scruffy light brown hair, wearing dirty grey jogging pants and an equally dirty light blue T-shirt. J.J. ran to catch up with Derek.

But Mr. Schmidt stopped him at the door. "What's the hurry, J.J.?" he asked. "The bell hasn't rung yet. You know the rules."

"But — but —" J.J. stammered. Where was Derek? He took a deep breath. "We saw somebody in the classroom. With the lunches."

"Oh!" Mr. Schmidt took off with quick steps. J.J. practically had to run to keep up.

They found Derek inspecting his lunch.

"*Derek Scott!*" Mr. Schmidt roared. "What are you doing in the classroom during recess?"

"*No!*" J.J. yelped. "Derek saw him too! Then he ran inside and —"

"I wasn't messing with the lunches," Derek agreed.

"And what were you doing this very moment?" demanded Mr. Schmidt.

"Checking my lunch," Derek said sheepishly. "He didn't take anything."

None of Miss Davis's students had any problems with their lunches that day. But a girl from Mr. Schmidt's class let out a loud scream when she opened her lunchbox. Half the students in the room got up to look at the cigarette butts. Shaun chose that minute to start throwing his yogurt around the room. Mr. Schmidt had a hard time settling everybody down. Shaun got a detention, and Mr. Schmidt looked suspiciously at J.J. and Derek.

J.J.'s mouth dropped open in dismay. "He thinks *we* had something to do with it?" he gasped.

"You and your stupid ideas," Derek mumbled.

So far, today hadn't been much better than yesterday. But still, J.J. *had* seen somebody in the classroom. So had Derek. Somehow they'd have to catch that criminal — and prove *they* were innocent!

Chapter 4

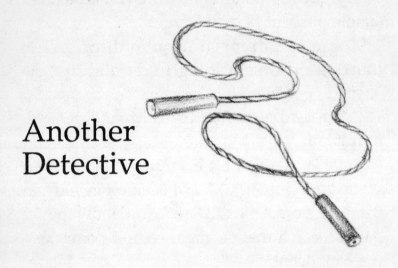

Another Detective

"I think we should forget about being detectives. If I get in trouble at school, I'll probably be grounded for a whole week," Derek complained after school that day. The two boys were riding their skateboards down Cameron Street, toward the river.

J.J. was baffled. "How can you talk about giving up? We saw the criminal. We almost caught him too — red-handed!" With a good strong push, he swerved and sent his skateboard up a driveway. Ka-CHUK, ka-CHUK, ka-CHUK. It glided over the cracks in the sidewalk like a train going down the tracks.

Tanya Webster was jumping rope on the sidewalk two houses away. So was her little sister Amy, but she kept tripping on her rope.

"Here I come!" yelled J.J. "Look out!"

"*You* look out," said Tanya, never missing a skip.

J.J. rolled closer. "Here comes the famous lunchbox detective," he said. "Let him through in the name of the law!"

Tanya didn't budge. Her chin stuck out. "Sidewalks are for pedestrians. You've got wheels, so you go in the street."

"Huh," said Derek, and rolled up onto the sidewalk too.

Tanya glared at the boys. "You know what you'll get if you hurt me or my sister," she threatened.

J.J. had a feeling he *did* know. He dragged his

toe on the concrete and stopped his skateboard. "Man, that was cool what you did to Shaun!" he said. "I'm going to get my mom to let me take karate too." Although when he'd mentioned the idea, his mom hadn't seemed terribly impressed.

"I'm already signed up," Derek boasted. J.J. had a feeling he was lying.

"Hey Tanya," said J.J., changing the subject. "We saw the lunchbox criminal at work today."

Derek scowled. "And *we* got in trouble."

"You *saw* him?" Tanya said at the same instant. "Who was it?"

"I don't know," said J.J., puzzled. "I couldn't really recognize him. It wasn't Shaun."

"I can jump rope," Tanya's sister Amy said proudly.

J.J. sighed. Sometimes little sisters could be such a pain.

Tanya seemed to think so too. "Who wants to jump rope?" she said. "Go play someplace else, Amy."

"Noooooo," whined Amy.

"I'll let you have three pieces of my Mega-bubble gum," Tanya offered in an extra-nice voice.

Amy thought it over for a minute. "OK," she said, and skipped away.

"You *saw* him?" Tanya asked again in a low voice. "We'd'd better make plans! To trap him."

J.J. looked at Derek.

"Huh," said Derek. "Who said we wanted a girl on our team?"

Tanya looked hurt. Suddenly J.J. remembered the way she'd gone after Shaun. "We need Tanya," he said. "She has a special talent." Even so, he gave Tanya a good hard look. "You'll help keep Shaun away?" he asked.

"I'll think about it," Tanya replied.

They all looked at each other suspiciously.

"Come on," said J.J. "To the hideout."

"*What?*" Derek yelped. "You'd give away our hideout?"

"We've got to be professional," said J.J. "Tanya won't give away our secret." He gave her another hard look. "You'd better not."

"Cross my heart, and hope to die, stick a needle in my eye," promised Tanya.

J.J. believed her. He pushed off with his skateboard. "Away to catch the criminal!" he cried.

Derek followed, leaving Tanya running hard to keep up.

"That's not fair!" Tanya panted as she caught up with them at the river.

"Huh," said Derek. "Get a skateboard."

Tanya's chin jutted out. "You just wait. I *will*."

J.J. began climbing the steep grassy dike that had been built along the river to prevent flooding. "We'll be like real private eyes," he said. "We'll look for clues and —"

But Derek wasn't listening. "Girls can't skateboard," he said as they skittered downhill again toward the clump of willows that was their hideout.

"Who says?" demanded Tanya.

"I do," Derek said.

J.J. ducked into the narrow hollow between the willow branches and the river bank. Just for a moment he was alone in a private green world of leaves and branches. Here and there he could peek through and see the glint of water.

Then the green walls swayed with a crashing sound. Derek's head appeared. "I can't get any detentions," he warned.

Tanya's eyes glowed as she followed Derek into the hideout. "This is awesome!" she whispered. "We can see out and nobody can see us!"

"That's the idea," J.J. said impatiently. It was crowded with three people in the hideout. He was beginning to wonder if it had been such a good idea to include Tanya.

"We should trap him," Tanya went on. "You know, in the act."

"How?" asked Derek, crouching low beneath the branches.

"We rig it somehow," whispered Tanya, "so anyone who moves a lunchbox will get caught. Let me think."

J.J. swatted at mosquitos while Tanya sat thinking.

"Cans!" she shouted.

J.J. and Derek both jumped.

"Tin cans!" Tanya said again.

"What are you talking about?" asked J.J.

But as Tanya explained her plan, it almost sounded as if it would work — as long as the lunchbox criminal struck in their own classroom again.

Chapter 5

A Plan

J.J. felt pretty nervous the next morning. During reading time the whole class went to the library. Miss Davis wanted them to practice looking things up in the card catalogue and finding books on the shelves.

J.J. crossed his fingers for luck. So far everything looked good. Everybody was busy and Miss Davis was talking to Mrs. Bourassa, the librarian. J.J. went over to them. "Miss Davis?

I forgot my library book. Can I get it from my desk?"

Miss Davis reminded him to be quiet in the hall and then had to go see about Kyle, who was bouncing his eraser off the globe.

J.J. sucked in a deep breath and darted out the back doors. He and Tanya had hidden their backpacks in the bushes because they were pretty smelly. J.J. held his nose and grabbed the backpacks, then crept inside.

Tanya came out of the girls' washroom. J.J. tried to hurry toward the classroom, but each time he did, the backpacks made a clanking noise.

"Shh," Tanya hissed.

They tiptoed to the classroom. J.J. got his library book out of his desk, so he wouldn't be lying. Now it was up to Derek. Derek's job was to find ways of keeping Miss Davis busy — if Kyle didn't!

"Hurry!" whispered Tanya. "Oh, this has to work!"

J.J. unfastened the backpacks. With a clatter,

empty cans tumbled out and rolled around on the floor — soup cans, juice cans, sardine cans. A ravioli can had some eggshell stuck inside. A dribble of Coke spilled out of a pop can that Derek had found on the way to school.

"Yuck!" they both said at once.

The whole plan depended on the cans fitting into the cupboard right over the luchbox shelf. J.J. moved Kamran Patel's desk to the back of the room and climbed onto it so he could look inside the cupboard.

"Is there enough room?" Tanya whispered. She was unwinding a ball of string.

"Just barely." J.J. jumped down. Quickly he started tossing the cans into plastic grocery bags from Tanya's backpack. How long would Derek be able to keep Miss Davis from noticing that J.J. and Tanya hadn't come back to the library? Or what if Kyle got in so much trouble Miss Davis decided to bring him back to the classroom?

"Hurry up!" Tanya said again. With the string she made a giant loop that ran through the handles of all the lunchboxes.

The classroom was starting to smell from all the empty cans. Would Miss Davis notice if they opened some windows? J.J. knew she'd notice the smell for sure, though, if he didn't let some fresh air in.

"Someone's coming!" Tanya gasped.

Footsteps echoed in the far end of the hall. Was it Miss Davis? Or maybe Mrs. Markoski?

As fast as he could, J.J. tied the loose ends of string through the handles of the grocery bags. He climbed back up on Kamran's desk, and stuffed the bulging bags into the cupboard. Beneath him, Tanya was tying the same strings to the loop that connected all the lunchboxes.

The footsteps kept coming closer. . . .

J.J. pushed the cupboard door so it was almost shut. But when he jumped down, he brushed against one of the strings. Some of the cans clattered to the floor. The sound was loud in the quiet room.

"What did you do that for?" Tanya hissed.

"You and your dumb ideas!" J.J. said. "If you

don't like the way I'm doing it, then do it yourself." J.J.'s hands shook as he put the cans back. He practically ran as he shoved Kamran's desk back to the right place.

The footsteps kept coming closer, closer — and then they stopped.

J.J. sighed with relief. Trembling, he picked up his library book. "Don't forget to cut the string before lunch," he warned.

Tanya nodded. "We'd be in *big* trouble!"

Miss Davis was looking at Derek's notebook when J.J. and Tanya crept into the library. Derek's face was red. J.J. put the library book in the return box and went to work.

Miss Davis crinkled her nose when the class came back to the classroom. "What's that funny smell?" she asked.

J.J.'s heart was beating so hard he was sure Miss Davis would hear it.

"I don't smell anything," Tanya said.

"*I* do," said Kyle. He made throwing-up noises.

"That's enough, Kyle," Miss Davis said.

"Class, get out your science books."

J.J. grinned at Tanya and Derek. The trap was set!

But there was one thing they hadn't counted on. Ginny Chen came in late. She was carrying her lunchbox.

Suddenly J.J. felt as if he had grasshoppers jumping around inside. There wasn't much space on the lunchbox shelf. Ginny would have to move some kids' lunches so she could put hers away. He swallowed hard and looked at Tanya. They had to keep Ginny away from the trap! Tanya was already heading for the back of the room.

It was too late.

CRASH!

There were screams, and Ginny and Tanya jumped out of the way. Cans rolled everywhere. Some went up the aisles between the desks. A sardine can stopped right by Kyle's foot. Kyle kicked it away and climbed on top of his desk to get away from the smell.

Everyone was laughing, except J.J. and

Tanya. Their faces were bright red.

And then Miss Davis was standing up. "All right," she said in the terrible and quiet voice she used when she was *really* mad. "Class, who is responsible for this?" She looked right at J.J., and then at Tanya. She sounded almost scarier than Mrs. Markoski.

By recess time, J.J. was beginning to wish that he and Tanya *had* been sent to Mrs. Markoski, instead of being punished by Miss Davis. He had a feeling Mrs. Markoski would find out, anyhow. When the other kids lined up to go outside, J.J. and Tanya each got several sheets of paper. After the doorway cleared, they went to sit in the hall with paper, their pens, and some Superwhite.

"This is going to take *forever!*" Tanya groaned.

"Think I don't already know that?" J.J. muttered. That Tanya, always getting him in trouble! It was going to take *longer* than forever to write *I am not a detective. The teachers will solve the problem*, 100 times. And Miss Davis had said very clearly that there were to be no spelling or punctuation errors. Worse yet, the 100 lines had to be turned in by tomorrow morning.

Already J.J.'s hand was beginning to ache. At this rate it would take all *year* to finish the lines! And then Tanya looked over his shoulder and pointed out some mistakes. J.J. groaned and reached for the Superwhite.

He almost didn't pay attention when somebody walked by. All he saw was a raggedy pair of blue running shoes and legs in dirty grey jogging pants. For an instant there was the smell of stale tobacco smoke in the air.

"Who was that?" Tanya whispered, jabbing J.J. with her elbow.

"Quit jiggling me!" J.J. said furiously. "See what you made me do?" He jabbed Tanya back.

And then the fire alarm went off.

In one way J.J. was relieved. Now he wouldn't have to spend his whole recess writing. On the other hand, he'd have to do it all during lunch and after school. Without waiting for Tanya, he grabbed his paper and pen. Let Tanya carry the Superwhite — see if he cared!

Outside, everybody was lining up in their usual places. But the teachers looked kind of confused.

"I smell smoke!" Ginny Chen whispered to somebody as J.J. went by.

As usual, Shaun was goofing around in line. "School's burning," he said with his crazy laugh. And then he bumped into Lisa Perreault.

"*Shaun Higgins!*" Mr. Schmidt thundered. "You will come and stand with me."

Shaun gave him an "I don't care" look and went to the head of the line. But as he did so, he tripped J.J. The papers slipped and spilled. Shaun walked all over J.J.'s lines, leaving muddy footprints across the writing.

"HEY!" J.J. yelled. "You wrecked my lines! You're going to pay for this, or else!" he muttered as he picked up the papers.

"Or else what?" Shaun said with an ugly grin.

Tanya scurried into line behind J.J. "I saw somebody!" she whispered. "You know the kid who walked past when we were writing? He went into the classrooms! I saw him, after the fire drill started, and —"

"*Quietly*, Tanya," said Miss Davis, grasping Tanya by the elbow and leading her to the front of the line.

"Think I care?" J.J. muttered to no one in particular.

He stood there feeling mad as the teachers checked attendance. Maybe there really *was* a fire. Fire drills never lasted this long.

"I hear sirens!" whispered Kyle.

But then the bell rang, at last, and they had to go back inside. J.J. crumpled his messed-up lines and tossed them into the garbage as he walked past. "Think I care?" he said again.

But by lunch time he cared. He brought a clean sheet of paper along with him, and started writing even before he opened his lunchbox.

But he was too hungry to work on his lines.

He opened his lunchbox — and yelled.

The criminal had struck again.

"It's not *fair!*" J.J. complained as he took his lunchbox to show it to Mr. Schmidt. "*Twice!* Why does he always have to pick on me?"

But as it turned out, J.J. wasn't the only victim this time. In all, ten children's lunches had been stolen. Tanya's was missing. So was Ginny Chen's. Several victims were from Ms. Eaton-Cook's and Mr. Schmidt's classes. The only good thing about it, J.J. decided, was that at last Shaun's lunch was missing too.

They all went to sit in the nurse's office with Mrs. Markoski while Miss Davis went out to buy hamburgers for everyone.

"We saw the criminal," Tanya said in an important voice. "He had light brown hair, kinda scraggly, and a dirty light blue T-shirt, and grey jogging pants."

"And holey blue running shoes," J.J. added, remembering.

Mrs. Markoski looked extremely puzzled. "You're absolutely certain?" she asked.

"He was going into the classrooms!" Tanya insisted. "After the fire alarm went."

"And he smelled like old smoke!" J.J. said suddenly.

But Mrs. Markoski was still talking. "Does anybody here know anything about why the fire alarm happened to go off today?"

Nobody knew, not even Shaun, not even when Mrs. Markoski asked them to think hard. An electric silence quivered in the air.

"There was no fire drill planned for today," Mrs. Markoski said in a low, ominous voice. "If anybody here knows anything about it, I will need to know. Immediately."

The idea shot into J.J. like a laser bolt. Quickly he looked at Tanya. "The criminal!" he said. "I bet he made the alarm go off —"

"— so he could get more lunches," Tanya finished up.

Mrs. Markoski's mouth tightened. But before she had a chance to say anything else, the door opened. Miss Davis walked in carrying two big bags.

J.J.'s mouth watered at the tantalizing smell. Hamburgers! He was so hungry he could hardly wait.

"Wish I could get my lunch stolen every day," Shaun said. "This sure beats peanut butter."

J.J. could see his point. Quickly he began unwrapping the wonderful warm hamburger in his hands.

But Tanya jabbed him in the ribs again, before he even had a chance to take his first bite. "Get it?" she hissed. "Nobody was missing from the fire drill. That means somebody else is coming into this school and stealing our lunches!"

Chapter 6

More Things Go Wrong

"If you think you're so smart, then solve the problem yourself!" J.J. yelled into the telephone that evening. Then he slammed the phone down. He was sick of the mystery of the lunchbox criminal. He was sick of Tanya. Now she was even calling him at home! And he still had 69 lines to write. *I am not a detective. The teachers will solve the problem.* He was sick of the lines, that was for sure! Let the teachers solve the problem. Or let Tanya do it. He didn't care.

Mom was busy working on a big project for one of her classes. Jessica was howling in her playpen. J.J. decided to drive his Z-28 around the house. But the car didn't go very fast over the carpet, so he moved into the kitchen. Radical! That was more like it! The car zoomed past the refrigerator and then shot under the table. Oops! It crashed into a chair leg. It crashed so hard the batteries fell out and rolled across the kitchen floor.

"J.J.!" his mom yelled. "Please! Can't you try to keep quiet while I'm studying? Why don't you go play in your room until supper time?"

"When are we eating?" J.J. asked meekly. After all, it was past 6:00 and as far as he could tell, nothing was cooking.

"Oh no!" Mom said. "Supper — I haven't even thought about it."

"I can fix supper," J.J. offered. "I can make hot dogs in the microwave."

"Would you *really*, J.J.?" Mom appeared in the doorway holding Jessica. "You're an angel."

J.J. didn't want to be an angel, but he did want supper. He was considering suggesting that if he fixed supper, maybe Mom could do some lines for him — but he decided he'd better not.

Mom put Jessica back in her playpen. Right away Jessica started screaming.

"Can't we make her stop?" asked J.J.

"I wish," said Mom. Suddenly she was talking to him almost as if he were a grownup. That felt kind of good.

"Maybe she's hungry," J.J. suggested.

"Oh, heavens!" cried Mom. "I missed her afternoon snack."

You missed mine too, thought J.J. But he didn't say it. He said instead, "The lunchbox criminal stole my lunch again, and other kids' lunches too, so Miss Davis bought hamburgers for everybody."

"Would you mind giving Jessica a piece of

cheese?" Mom asked. "And a cut-up apple."

"Hey!" said J.J. "I said, my *lunch* was . . ." But he stopped. Mom wasn't really listening, and now he had to take care of Jessica too! He cut up some cheese and an apple, and dropped the pieces into the playpen. Jessica screeched and laughed and crawled over to get them. Now she smelled like she had a messy diaper — but Mom hadn't said anything about changing diapers, so J.J. figured he didn't need to do anything about it.

He walked away and put his lines on the kitchen table. While he waited for the microwave oven to buzz, he wrote a little bit. He kept his lines on the table while they ate, so he could write between bites.

That was a terrible mistake.

Even though Jessica was strapped in her high chair, that didn't prevent disaster. For some reason Jessica decided to throw her plate. It was full of cut-up pieces of hot dog, strained carrots, and lots of applesauce that Mom had given her. The whole plate landed right on top of J.J.'s lines. Upside down.

J.J. felt like tipping over the high chair.

"Now I'll have to do them all over again!" he wailed.

Mom hugged him, and then got busy wiping the carrots and applesauce off the lines.

"Stupid —"

But Mom put her hand over J.J.'s mouth and then went to answer the telephone. J.J. put his head down on the table.

"That was Miss Davis," said Mom when she got back to the table. "She has decided that you don't need to write any more lines. She said the teachers and the principal are all going to work very hard to solve the problem of the stolen lunches."

"Oh," said J.J., glad that he didn't have to finish the lines. But he was disappointed too. Why *couldn't* he and Derek — and Tanya, he guessed — solve the mystery all on their own?

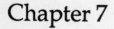

Chapter 7

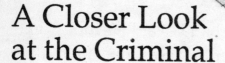

A Closer Look at the Criminal

By the next morning J.J. had figured out what they had to do. He and Derek — and Tanya — would have to race the teachers to see who could solve the mystery first. He was trying to explain this to the others as the class lined up for an assembly, but everybody else kept talking.

"I think the assembly's about bicycle safety," Ginny Chen said.

"I bet it's about *tricycle* safety," Kyle snickered.

"Remember the jugglers we saw last time?" said Michael Strongchild. "They were excellent!"

"We've got to race the teachers!" J.J. whispered to Derek for the third time.

"Huh?" said Derek loudly.

"Quiet down, class!" Miss Davis sounded kind of tired. "We aren't going anywhere until it's so quiet we can hear a pin drop."

"What kind of pin?" asked Kyle. "A bowling pin?"

Miss Davis gave Kyle a look that made him extra quiet.

"We have to race the teachers!" J.J. whispered again.

"Oh, I get it!" Tanya said. "To see who —"

"Will you quit eavesdropping?" said J.J. "I'm talking to Derek."

"*Class!*" Miss Davis said again. "If you don't quiet down right now, we won't be having any gym today."

Suddenly it was quiet. *Very* quiet.

J.J. thought he saw the lunchbox criminal again as they were all going into the gym for assembly. He was walking along with Ms. Eaton-Cook's class, pretending to be part of it. Why couldn't their line go faster, and pass Ms. Eaton-Cook's class? Then he could at least get a good look at the criminal's face. But the line moved along at its usual slow speed.

What could he do? The criminal was right there! All he'd have to do would be to run out of line, just for a moment. He recognized that scruffy light brown hair, those jogging pants, the runners, the dirty light blue T-shirt. Nobody else realized it, not even Derek. The problem was, how to catch the criminal without any help from the teachers?

All the classes kept on going toward the gym. So did the lunchbox criminal. J.J. stared hard at his back — that was the geek who'd stolen his lunch *twice*, who'd put filthy cigarette butts in his lunchbox. What could he do? It had to be something that wouldn't get him in trouble, and he'd have to do it quickly, because Ms. Eaton-Cook's class was just about to go into the gym, and they sat on the opposite side of the room. What was the criminal going to do, sit through assembly just like every other kid? Wouldn't people notice him?

J.J. had the idea just as they were passing the bulletin board. Lots of notices were stapled to the board right by his shoulder. Quickly J.J. tore one off and folded it into a paper airplane. He aimed it at the criminal's back. He didn't miss.

The criminal turned around.

It was a girl.

J.J. was so surprised that he forgot to walk when the line started moving again, and everybody bumped into him. How could the criminal be a *girl?* But he was sure he hadn't been mistaken. That proud, skinny face looked tough, and he could see why they'd thought it was a boy at first. When he looked again, the criminal was gone.

The assembly was long and boring, and Mrs.

Markoski talked a lot about the stolen lunches. J.J. kept turning his head, trying to see if the criminal was in the gym, until Miss Davis finally pulled him out to the aisle and gave him a talking-to. J.J. didn't really listen.

Was the criminal in the gym? What would she think, hearing herself talked about in front of the whole school? J.J. was sure she wouldn't like it!

No lunches were missing that day.

It was almost disappointing. And because tomorrow was Saturday, J.J. knew he'd have to wait until Monday to do anything.

Chapter 8

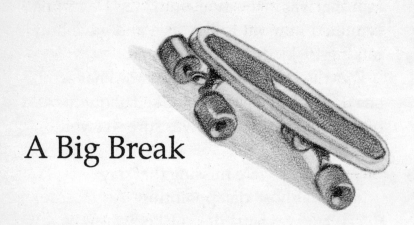

A Big Break

When he'd finished watching cartoons the next morning, J.J. skateboarded to the river to meet Derek. In the distance, J.J. could see Tanya delivering flyers. And there was her little sister Amy, jumping rope like always. He'd have to disappear into the hideout before Tanya came too close. After finding out that the criminal was a girl, Tanya had been even *more* interested in solving the mystery — and J.J. didn't really feel like talking to Tanya right now.

J.J. waited for Derek to show up. He was late as usual so J.J. tucked his skateboard under his arm and pushed through the branches. A mosquito kept whining in his ear. He swatted it. Branches scratched his bare arms.

Suddenly, he heard a rustling in the hideout. "Derek," he groaned. "Why didn't you tell me you were here already? I've been waiting half the —"

"Whatcha doing, Jeremy ratface?"

Shaun! J.J. backed out as fast as he could. This was a total disaster! If Shaun knew their hideout, they were dead meat!

Branches swayed wildly as Shaun came after him. "Nobody invades my fort and gets away with it!" he yelled.

J.J. took a deep breath once he was on open ground. "It's not *your* fort. We found it first."

"It is now," Shaun said. His foot wrapped around J.J.'s ankle, bringing him down and sending the skateboard rolling. J.J. landed hard on his chin.

He said some bad words as he got up.

But Shaun just laughed — and then made a run for J.J.'s skateboard.

"Hey!" yelled J.J. "That's mine! You leave it alone!"

"Try and make me," Shaun taunted with an ugly grin. He held the skateboard to his chest.

J.J. grabbed for the skateboard. Shaun pushed and caught him off balance. J.J. teetered. Then he was sliding down the bank toward the river. Behind him he heard a rustling in the weeds. Before he realized what was happening, his skateboard shot past him, bumping crazily over the clumps of dirt and weeds.

J.J. threw himself at the skateboard, but it was too late. The skateboard bounced, flipped, and then splashed into the river and sank. J.J. could hardly believe what had happened. He screamed more words at Shaun, but again, Shaun just laughed.

And then there was a familiar yell.

There was Tanya, advancing toward Shaun.

"Stay out of this, Tanya," J.J. yelled. "This is between Shaun and me!"

But Tanya ignored him and kept on coming. *Deadly!* thought J.J. If he hadn't been so furious about his skateboard and the hideout, he really would've enjoyed watching Tanya.

Shaun kicked out at Tanya. But Tanya somehow wasn't quite where Shaun expected her to be. There was another yell, and then Shaun went flying. He landed like a sack full of scrap metal. Tanya sat on him.

"I saw what you did, you bully!" she screamed at him. "You'll pay."

Shaun was on the ground, squirming. J.J. nearly laughed out loud. He started back up the river bank so he'd have a better view. But then Shaun wriggled free. As the bully scrambled to his feet, he caught Tanya in a headlock. "Think you can mess with me?" he said, sneering. He tightened his grip and Tanya started choking.

J.J. gulped and broke into a run. He'd have to do something, or Tanya might get hurt.

Things didn't work out quite the way he'd hoped. Suddenly J.J. was in the middle of a tangle of arms and legs. Something hit him in the face. His nose felt as if it had been smashed right into his head. Then blood was running down his shirt. He saw Shaun's face right in front of him, and socked him in the eye.

"You kids!"

The voice sounded far away, but suddenly J.J. realized he'd been hearing it for a while. There was Mrs. Peterson, looking like an evil space monster. He saw a hand clamp down at the back of Shaun's neck, and then something yanked him backwards too.

"You kids!" Mrs. Peterson shouted. "Always fighting. At this rate you'll land in jail before you even get out of grade school."

"He started it!" J.J. yelled. Mrs. Peterson's grip on his neck felt like iron.

Mrs. Peterson didn't seem to care who had started it. She shook him and Shaun. "Your parents are going to hear about this," she threatened.

"It's not J.J.'s fault!" Tanya cried. "Shaun threw J.J.'s skateboard in the river. I saw him."

But Mrs. Peterson just glared at her.

J.J. felt like socking Mrs. Peterson too. Now he was in trouble all over again. Mom was still working on her paper for her class, and if she saw him like *this*, he'd be banished to his room for the rest of his life! Or at least until it was time to get Dad at the airport.

Besides the blood on his shirt, J.J. could feel his lip swelling up like a hot air balloon. It felt like it was as big as half his face. Could a fat lip pop? Then he'd probably have to go to the hospital to get it fixed, and he'd have to wear a giant bandage, and then everybody at school would stare at him.

J.J.'s mom *was* angry, but not quite the way Mrs. Peterson expected. She dropped her books onto a chair and her mouth went into a hard, tight line.

She sent J.J. upstairs to the bathroom to wash his face and change his shirt. When he came down again, Mom was sitting by the telephone. Jessica was whining in the playpen.

"Where does Shaun live?" Mom asked.

"Angus Crescent," J.J. said. "Why?" He stared in surprise at his mother. What was she going to do, march over to see Shaun's mom, and beat *her* up?

But Mom opened the telephone book instead and told J.J. to take Jessica for a walk in the stroller.

"Do I have to?" complained J.J.

"Take your baby sister for a walk," his mom said in a "do not argue with me" voice. "She needs a change of scenery and some fresh air."

J.J. knew better than to argue.

He hadn't gone very far when he heard running footsteps behind him.

"J.J.! Wait!" It was Derek.

J.J. kept going, but a moment later Derek had caught up. "Man!" said Derek. "What happened to your face, huh?"

J.J. scowled. "What happened to your *hair?*" he asked. It was obvious Derek had been to the barbershop, but J.J. wanted to rub it in. "What took you so long? I waited and you never showed up. Shaun was in our hideout, and he sank my skateboard in the river!"

"That geek!" cried Derek. "We'll have to get him for that."

"I already did," J.J. told him. "I pounded him." J.J. was starting to enjoy himself. He made his fat lip stick out a little further.

Derek looked impressed.

"Hey! Guys!" It was Tanya calling them.

"Oh no!" said J.J.

"Ey-YEH!" screeched Jessica. She threw her rattle onto Mr. MacDonald's lawn. The sprinkler was going.

"Jessica!" J.J. snapped. He knew if he just left the rattle there, he'd get in trouble. So he darted into the sprinkler and got his clean shirt all wet.

"Guys, I said *wait!*"

Darn! Tanya had caught up with them, and worse yet, little Amy wasn't far behind, with her jump rope trailing along the sidewalk. Tanya had a place on her cheek that looked pretty sore.

"We really got *him*," Tanya said smugly.

"Huh?" said Derek. "Got who?"

"Shaun," Tanya said even more smugly.

"*Huh?*" said Derek.

"My mom's phoning his mom right now," J.J. added, to change the subject. There was a little quiver in his stomach. Would Mom get the Higginses to buy him a new skateboard? Or make Shaun fish his old one out of the river?

"What happened?" asked Derek.

"I *told* you," J.J. said irritably. "You wouldn't have missed it if you hadn't been a hundred years late."

But Tanya started telling Derek all about the showdown.

Meanwhile, Jessica kept on babbling.

"I saw too," Amy said proudly. She blew a big bubble of gum.

"Get lost," said Tanya.

Amy ignored her big sister. "What a cute baby!" she said, after sealing the bubble so it wouldn't leak. She bent over to look at Jessica.

"Mmmmgah DEE!" cried Jessica. She

grabbed for the big pink bubble. It popped all over Amy's face and stuck to Jessica's fingers, besides.

"*Jessica!*" said J.J. But he couldn't help laughing — even though it made his face hurt.

"Serves you right, Amy," said Tanya. "Always showing off with your gum."

"I don't care," Amy said. "Gillian blows bubbles all the time."

"Oh now she's talking about her imaginary friend," groaned Tanya. "She says this kid lives in the school, and she shares her lunches with her."

"She's not imaginary!" Amy cried. "She's *real*. She doesn't have any home, and —"

"Oh sure," said Tanya. "Go jump rope, OK?"

"Look!" Amy said, pointing at Jessica.

Jessica was staring, mesmerized, at a ladybug that was crawling on the back of her hand. Then, with no warning, Jessica screeched and popped the ladybug into her mouth.

"Oh, yuck!" Derek groaned. "*Gross!*"

J.J. didn't know what to do. Were ladybugs

poisonous? What if Jessica *died,* and it was all his fault? "I better get Mom," he said.

"It won't hurt her," Tanya said. "I remember when Amy ate a fly."

"Ughhh!" said Derek. "I think I'm going to be sick."

J.J. felt the same way. "Are you *sure?*" he asked, looking hard at Tanya.

"Would I lie? Of course I'm sure," Tanya replied.

"Gillian said she swallowed a mosquito once by mistake," Amy offered.

"Can't you be quiet? We're not interested in imaginary friends," Tanya said.

Amy pouted. Gum was still stuck to her nose. She stomped her foot. "How many times do I have to tell you?" she yelled, getting red in the face. "Gillian's not imaginary! She lives in the school with her big sister and her sister gets lunches . . . " And then Amy clapped both hands over her mouth as if she'd just done something awful.

Suddenly it was very quiet.

"The criminal!" J.J. gasped.

"OH!" said Tanya and Derek at the same instant. Their eyes looked as big as doughnuts.

"Our first big break in the case!" said J.J., excited.

"No!" cried Amy. "Don't tell! I'll get in trouble! *Gillian* will get in trouble! Roxanne will be really mad."

Jessica shouted and screeched just because everybody else was making so much noise.

Amy looked very little and very scared. "Don't tell!" she begged again. "I promised not to — "

"Now you just *un*-promised," Tanya said in a bossy big sister voice. "I'll give you all my packs of Mega-bubble if you help us."

"No," said Amy. Then she hesitated. "How many packs do you have?"

"Three," said Tanya.

Amy shook her head. "No. I can't get Gillian in trouble. Her sister said if she told —"

"I'll *buy* you gum," Derek offered.

Jessica squealed and spat up. J.J. wiped her chin. The ladybug had not come out. At a time

like this, why did he have to take care of his baby sister?

"I'll buy you *five* packs of Mega-bubble," Tanya wheedled. "And ten red licorice."

Amy shook her head again.

"Can't you just help us?" J.J. asked. "Please? I'm tired of getting my lunch stolen."

"Me too," Tanya agreed. "It's not fair to all the other kids at school either."

"But they all have homes," Amy argued. "And moms who give them food, and clothes."

"You better help us," Tanya threatened. "I'll tell Mom, and then she'll tell Mrs. Markoski."

Amy got very quiet.

"I'll buy you a Barbie," Tanya went on. "With my own money."

Amy got even quieter.

"Gom ging," said Jessica, and gave Amy a radiant smile.

"They ran away," Amy said in a tiny voice. "Because they didn't have any house or any food and their dad drinks and doesn't even care."

J.J. took a deep breath. One or two missing lunches was nothing compared to no house and no food. Or a dad who didn't even care about them.

"What about their mom?" he asked. "Why doesn't she help?"

"She died," said Amy. "A long time ago."

"Oh," Tanya said in a quiet voice.

"I know!" said Derek. "We'll help them take lunches."

J.J. didn't think that was such a good idea. "We'd get in trouble," he said. "And with all the teachers trying to find the criminal too, they'll just get caught anyhow."

Amy started crying.

"We'll help them," Tanya said. "We *have* to. But how?"

Chapter 9

Meeting
the Criminal

When J.J.'s dad got home from the conference that night they all went out to the
Italian Galleon for dinner. While they were
eating, J.J. asked him what happened to kids
who had no homes. His dad had talked about
social workers and foster parents. J.J. wasn't so
sure Roxanne would want that kind of help.

By Monday morning J.J. still had only vague
ideas about what they could do to help Gillian

and her sister.

One thing about being back at school was pretty awesome. J.J.'s fat lip had gone down, but Shaun had *two* black eyes! People were beginning to find out how he'd gotten them. Shaun walked around with his head down and didn't bug anybody much.

As they lined up to go into the building, Tanya came rushing over to them, followed by Amy and a scraggly little girl in dirty, raggedy clothes. "This is Gillian," Tanya puffed. "She said she'd help us talk to Roxanne."

"We brought extra lunches today," Amy said proudly. "Tanya made them, and Mom didn't even notice."

J.J. looked at Gillian. She was skinny and seemed scared. He wondered if she'd get in trouble for telling the secret. "We'll meet at recess," he said. "Behind the tunnels." After that they couldn't talk because the line of kids started going inside, and teachers were listening.

They had reading and science before recess. It seemed to take forever. J.J. kept wondering where the "criminal" — Roxanne — was. How could they *live* in the school? Did they sleep on the cots in the nurse's office? How come nobody had caught them?

"J.J." Miss Davis's voice penetrated his thoughts. "For the second time, can you tell us the name of the hot liquid inside the earth that makes volcanoes?"

"Huh?" J.J. gulped. All around him hands were waving in the air.

"I know!" cried Tanya. "It's —"

"MAGMA," J.J. said loudly.

"Thank you, J.J.," Miss Davis said. "I thought maybe you weren't listening."

When was the bell going to ring?

How on earth were they going to get Roxanne to come talk to them? They couldn't stalk her like prey and then jump on her. Especially with teachers everywhere. Amy seemed to know Gillian pretty well. Maybe they could pretend to kidnap Gillian and take her to the tunnels and Roxanne would see and follow them.

"J.J."

Miss Davis again! "Huh?" he said. Now he was beginning to sound like Derek.

"Would you care to come get the papers for your row?"

J.J. felt his face getting hot. How could Miss Davis figure out when he wasn't paying attention? She seemed to catch him every time.

"I have a plan!" he whispered as he passed Derek's desk. Across the aisle, Tanya listened too.

It seemed to take forever until recess.

Amy and Gillian were already jumping rope by the time J.J. and the others got outside. J.J. grabbed Amy's rope and ran. Amy shrieked and chased after him. Behind him he could hear more shrieks and several sets of running footsteps. He hoped the yard-duty teacher hadn't noticed. Crouching behind the concrete tunnels, he waited. Derek appeared, carrying another jump rope, followed by Tanya and the two little girls. "Shh!" said J.J., holding a finger to his lips. They waited.

One more set of footsteps came pounding toward them. An angry face peered around the tunnels and glared at them. "HEY! What are you doing to my little sister?" Roxanne demanded. She looked so mean that J.J. gulped. She looked even meaner than Shaun!

"It's OK," said Gillian.

"Are you kidding? They beat up on you and you say it's OK?"

J.J. took another deep breath. "We know about the lunches," he said. "We know what happened."

Roxanne grabbed Gillian's wrist. "Did you *tell?* I thought I could trust you!" She started dragging her sister off toward the fence. "I *told* you —"

Tanya started talking. Fast. "We know about the lunches. We want to help you guys. We brought more food for you."

Roxanne didn't seem too impressed. "We don't need your help," she said.

But Tanya wouldn't give up. She started talking again, asking where they were from, and telling them how brave they were for doing what they'd done.

Roxanne didn't seem to want to talk. "We're from Winnipeg," she said at last. "We're going to my aunt's. She lives somewhere near Vancouver."

"But how —?" J.J. broke off, baffled.

"We took the bus," Gillian said shyly. "Roxanne saved money from shovelling snow and cleaning people's yards. But there was only enough to buy tickets to Regina."

"What about the cigarette butts?" Tanya demanded. "That was really gross, you know, leaving them in people's lunchboxes."

"I smoke, OK?" Roxanne said in a tough voice.

"But why the lunchboxes?" Tanya was really angry. "And cigarettes cost money. Where'd you get it?"

"Think I'd tell you?" the other girl scoffed.

"Roxanne's mad," Gillian warned. "Don't get her madder. She doesn't like kids who have moms and homes and food. So she dumps her cigarette butts in lunchboxes."

J.J. couldn't think of anything to say. But Amy went right ahead and talked. "Smoking will give you cancer," she said.

"Who cares?" said Roxanne.

"Look!" Tanya said in a quiet voice. "We brought you extra food. Do you want it?"

Roxanne's chin began to quiver and her steely eyes suddenly looked watery. She turned away. Quickly Gillian ran over to hug her sister.

The bell rang.

J.J. did not feel like going back inside. But he could see Mrs. Markoski standing there with the yard-duty teacher. Now they couldn't even wait until the last minute. "You really should tell somebody," he said. "People will help."

Roxanne's chin jutted out. "We don't need anybody," she said.

But Gillian's face crumpled. She started to cry.

"Oh great," sighed Derek. "And we're going to be late too."

J.J. knew what he had to do. "We have to tell," he said. "So people can help you find your aunt."

Roxanne punched him in the stomach, so hard that he staggered backwards. But Mrs. Markoski had seen them, and was on her way over. Roxanne grabbed Gillian's hand and yanked. "Run! They'll call the cops!"

But Gillian wouldn't run. Instead, she just stood there looking at Amy. And J.J., Tanya, and Derek.

J.J. watched, dazed, as the principal confronted the two girls. Meanwhile, Mrs. Hoff was beckoning for the rest of them to come inside. J.J. turned and walked backwards, watching.

"Awesome," said Tanya. "Totally awesome! Could you imagine doing all that? Saving money to buy bus tickets, and then living in a *school?*"

"I could do that," Derek said. "Anybody could."

But J.J. wondered. He still was having

trouble imagining what it would be like to not have any house or food — or parents to take care of you. At that moment his heel bumped against the step. It was time to go inside.

Derek turned to J.J. "Hey!" he said. "I guess we solved the mystery, huh?"

"Right," J.J. agreed. It certainly hadn't turned out quite the way he'd expected, two homeless and hungry girls . . .

"I solved it too."

J.J. had forgotten all about Amy. But there she was, tagging along as usual.

"Huh," said Derek.

"She did," J.J. admitted, before Tanya could get mad at him.

"Come on!" Mrs. Hoff said impatiently. "You're late, all of you. And I can't even send you to the office, not at the moment."

Chapter 10

Some Answers

J.J. couldn't figure out what to do at recess the next morning. After spending all that time trying to solve the lunchbox mystery, the idea of just *playing* seemed kind of boring, somehow. Besides, he kept wondering what was happening to Roxanne and Gillian.

"Look at Shaun," Tanya said, laughing. "He still has his black eyes."

"I know," said J.J. In a way he almost felt

sorry for the bully. It couldn't be much fun to have to walk around school with everybody staring at you. He had a feeling Shaun's life might be kind of different from now on. So would Roxanne's and Gillian's, for sure. "I wish we knew what's going to happen to the criminal," he said.

"*Roxanne*, you dummy," Tanya corrected. "Yeah, me too. I hope they find their aunt. Wouldn't it be *awful* if they couldn't?"

"We're going to miss all the excitement," Derek said sadly.

"Unless we find another mystery!" Tanya's eyes sparkled.

"No way!" groaned J.J. It looked as if they were going to be stuck with Tanya for a while. Maybe if they avoided mysteries, she'd get bored and go play with some girls instead. On the other hand, it really had been kind of fun.

"Are we in trouble *again*?" Derek asked suddenly.

J.J. looked up. Mrs. Markoski was walking toward them.

"We didn't do anything this time," said Tanya. "We can't possibly be in trouble."

But even so, J.J.'s heart started beating in a scared, jumpy way.

"I thought the three of you might like to hear the news," the principal said. "The Children's Aid people have found the girls' aunt, and she's on a flight right now. She's been frantic with worry. She wants to take the girls home to live with her. And by the way, Roxanne said she was sorry for stealing the lunches and putting in cigarette butts. She said she'd try to quit smoking, too."

"Oh good!" said Tanya. Suddenly she was bouncing up and down with excitement.

A warm, quiet happiness grew inside J.J. "I'm glad they're going to be OK," he said. It just wasn't fair for kids to have it so rough. J.J. thought of his own family, a mom and dad who loved him — even baby Jessica wasn't so bad. He felt lucky.

Mrs. Markoski walked away and the bell rang.

"We really helped them!" Tanya kept saying as they went to line up.

"I know," said Derek. "We heard you the first time."

J.J. tried backing away from Tanya, but then he bumped against somebody.

It was Shaun.

The familiar prickly scared feeling that usually raced through J.J. was gone! And Shaun backed away and didn't say anything. Kyle was there, and he gave J.J. and Tanya a curious look — almost as if they were *dangerous!* There was a new skateboard at J.J.'s house, too. A bright orange and yellow Devastator. J.J. had spent all Sunday afternoon riding it around the neighbourhood.

J.J. laughed suddenly and jabbed Tanya in the ribs.

"Ow!" she yelled. "Quit it!"

"I got a new skateboard," J.J. boasted.

"We *know*," Derek groaned.

And then Tanya surprised J.J. "So have I," she said. "I'll catch up to you guys in no time."

"No way!" said Derek. "Girls can't skateboard!"

"Wanna bet?" asked Tanya with a dangerous look in her eyes.

"Huh," said Derek.

J.J. shook his head and went into the building. Without Tanya's help they might never have solved the mystery — and Shaun certainly wouldn't have those black eyes.

Just then his stomach growled. It was going to be a long wait until lunch. At least from now on he could be sure of finding *lunch* in his lunchbox.

They walked into the classroom. J.J. checked the shelf, just to make sure.

His lunchbox wasn't there.

"Hey!" he yelped. "Somebody stole my —" And then he remembered. His lunchbox was still sitting on top of the TV. He'd been in such a hurry to leave for school that morning he'd forgotten it.

"Oh no," J.J. groaned. "And it was pizza too!"